Are there pink dolphins in rivers?

Contents

Written by Tom Ottway

Illustrated by Alice N

Col.

What's in this book?

Listen and say

kangaroo

bird

turtle

fish

Download the audio at www.collins.co.uk/839672

parrot

snake

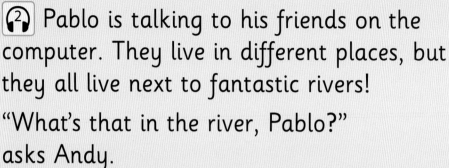 Pablo is talking to his friends on the computer. They live in different places, but they all live next to fantastic rivers!

"What's that in the river, Pablo?" asks Andy.

"Are they dolphins? Are they pink?" says Hilda.

Chapter 1 The Amazon River

Yes! We've got pink dolphins in my river!
I live next to the Amazon River.

It's a very long river. Everyone uses the river to travel to other towns.

We often see pink dolphins.
They're beautiful.

pink dolphin

long nose

lots of teeth

They can swim very fast. Sometimes we see them catch fish. Pink dolphins have very long noses and lots of teeth.

What animals are there in your river, Andy?

Chapter 2 The Mackenzie River

I live next to the Mackenzie River.
The Mackenzie River is the longest river in
my country.

In the winter, it's very cold, but very beautiful, too.

In the spring, there are lots of flowers.
The salmon come to the river.

And then brown bears come, too.
They catch the salmon and eat them.
Sometimes we can see big brown bears
from my house.

Are there brown bears in your river, Kylie?

salmon

Chapter 3 The Kennett River

This is the Kennett River. There aren't any brown bears. It's a small river, but lots of animals live next to it.

snake

king parrot

kangaroo

There's a very beautiful animal that lives here, too.

It's not easy to see platypuses! They sleep in the day and come out at night.
They swim and find food in the river.

platypus

What animals do you like in your river, Hilda?

Chapter 4 The Nile River

I live next to the Nile River.

A lot of birds live on the river. They catch fish from the river. They're beautiful.

My parents have got a boat and sometimes turtles swim next to the boat. I love them!

turtle

And sometimes we see hippos from my house.

They're very big! The hippos are my favourite animals in my river.

hippo

Picture dictionary

Listen and repeat

brown bear

catch fish

hippo

pink dolphin

platypus

river

spring

winter

1 Look and match

The Amazon River   The Mackenzie River

The Nile River   The Kennett River

2 Listen and say

Collins

Published by Collins
An imprint of HarperCollins*Publishers*
Westerhill Road
Bishopbriggs
Glasgow
G64 2QT

HarperCollins*Publishers*
1st Floor, Watermarque Building
Ringsend Road
Dublin 4
Ireland

William Collins' dream of knowledge for all began with the publication of his first book in 1819.

A self-educated mill worker, he not only enriched millions of lives, but also founded a flourishing publishing house. Today, staying true to this spirit, Collins books are packed with inspiration, innovation and practical expertise. They place you at the centre of a world of possibility and give you exactly what you need to explore it.

© HarperCollins*Publishers* Limited 2020

10 9 8 7 6 5 4 3 2

ISBN 978-0-00-839672-5

www.collins.co.uk/elt

British Library Cataloguing in Publication Data

A catalogue record for this publication is available from the British Library.

Author: Tom Ottway
Illustrator: Alice Negri (Beehive)
Series editor: Rebecca Adlard
Commissioning editor: Zoë Clarke
Publishing manager: Lisa Todd
Product managers: Jennifer Hall and Caroline Green
In-house editor: Alma Puts Keren
Project manager: Emily Hooton
Editor: Frances Amrani
Proofreaders: Natalie Murray and Michael Lamb
Cover designer: Kevin Robbins
Typesetter: 2Hoots Publishing Services Ltd
Audio produced by id audio, London
Reading guide author: Emma Wilkinson
Production controller: Rachel Weaver
Printed and bound by: GPS Group, Slovenia

Download the audio for this book and a reading guide for parents and teachers at www.collins.co.uk/839672